MIDLOTHIAN PUBLIC LIBRARY

3 1614 00167 2261

MIDLOTHIAN
PUBLIC LIBRARY

Ping Wants to Play

by Adam Gudeon

Holiday House / New York

MIDLOTHIAN PUBLIC LIBRARY
14701 S. KENTON AVE.
MIDLOTHIAN, IL 60445

To Ezra and Iris, my best pals

I LIKE TO READ is a registered trademark of Holiday House, Inc.

Copyright © 2014 by Adam Gudeon
All Rights Reserved
HOLIDAY HOUSE is registered in the U.S. Patent and Trademark Office.
Printed and Bound in March 2014 at Tien Wah Press, Johor Bahru, Johor, Malaysia.
The artwork was created with ink and digital coloring.
www.holidayhouse.com
First Edition
1 3 5 7 9 10 8 6 4 2

Library of Congress Cataloging-in-Publication Data
Gudeon, Adam.
Ping wants to play / by Adam Gudeon. — 1st ed.
p. cm. — (I like to read)
Summary: "Ping and Pong are friends, even though they like to do different things"—
Provided by publisher.
ISBN 978-0-8234-2854-0 (hardcover)
[1. Friendship—Fiction. 2. Individuality—Fiction. 3. Dogs—Fiction.] I. Title.
PZ7.G93495Pin 2014
[E]—dc23
2012039210

Ping and Pong are pals.

They eat together.

And they walk together.

Now Ping wants to play.
And Pong wants to nap.

Ping goes in.

And she comes out.
She is Super-Ping!

Super-Ping likes to run.

Pong likes to nap.

Super-Ping likes to jump.

Now Super-Ping will try to fly.

She runs.

She jumps.

Up she goes.

Where will she fall?

Super-Ping needs help.

Here comes Pong.

Pong likes to help.

That is why they are pals!

You will like these too!

Animals Work by Ted Lewin

Dinosaurs Don't, Dinosaurs Do by Steve Björkman
A NOTABLE SOCIAL STUDIES BOOK FOR YOUNG PEOPLE
AN IRA/CBC CHILDREN'S CHOICE

Fish Had a Wish by Michael Garland
KIRKUS REVIEWS BEST CHILDREN'S BOOK LIST
AND TOP 25 CHILDREN'S BOOKS LIST

The Fly Flew In by David Catrow
MARYLAND BLUE CRAB YOUNG READER AWARD WINNER

Moe Is Best by Richard Torrey

See Me Run by Paul Meisel
A THEODOR SEUSS GEISEL AWARD HONOR BOOK
AN ALA NOTABLE CHILDREN'S BOOK

Snow Joke by Bruce Degen

You Can Do It! by Betsy Lewin

See more I Like to Read® books.
Go to www.holidayhouse.com/I-Like-to-Read/